THE
STOPWATCH

WRITTEN BY
David Lloyd

ILLUSTRATED BY
Penny Dale

WALKER BOOKS

LONDON

Gran said, 'Here's a present, Tom.'

It was a stopwatch.

She started it. Tom stopped it.

It took him 9 seconds.

For Adam and Rosie
D.L.
For Bryan and Sarah
P.D.

Fun-to-Read Picture Books have been
grouped into three approximate readability
levels by Bernice and Cliff Moon. Yellow
books are suitable for beginners; red books
for readers acquiring first fluency; blue
books for more advanced readers.

This book has been assessed as Stage 7
according to *Individualised Reading*, by
Bernice and Cliff Moon, published by
The Centre for the Teaching of Reading,
University of Reading
School of Education.

First published 1986 by
Walker Books Ltd
184-192 Drummond Street
London NW1 3HP

Text © 1986 David Lloyd
Illustrations © 1986 Penny Dale

First printed 1986
Printed and bound by
L.E.G.O., Vicenza, Italy

British Library Cataloguing in Publication Data
Lloyd, David, *1945-*
The stopwatch.–(Fun-to-read picture books)
1. Readers–1950-
I. Title   II. Dale, Penny   III. Series
428'.6   PE1119

ISBN 0-7445-0529-1

Tom ran out of his gran's garden.

He ran home in 3 minutes 32 seconds.

He ate his tea in 2 minutes 6 seconds.

His sister Jan said

it was too disgusting to watch.

He got undressed and into the bath and
out again in 1 minute 43 seconds.

Jan said it was cheating not to use soap.

Next morning Tom held his breath
for 32 seconds.

He stood on his head for 11 seconds.

Jan said, 'Let's have a staring match.'

Tom lost.

He blinked after 41 seconds.

Then Tom lost his stopwatch.

He searched all over the house.

It took him a long time.

He didn't know how long because

he'd lost the stopwatch.

Jan came in.

She said, 'I can ride my bike to the shop,

eat an ice lolly, meet my friend,

go to the park, climb a tree,

eat another ice lolly and

ride home again in

32 minutes 58 seconds.'

Tom and Jan fought like cat and dog.

Just then Gran arrived.

She said, 'Stop that fighting!

Stop it at once!'

'Guess what, Gran,' Tom said.

'We just fought for exactly 7 minutes.'